The Wonder Book

by Amy Krouse Rosenthal

The Wonder

drawings by Paul Schmid

BOOK

HARPER

An Imprint of HarperCollinsPublishers

Dedicated to my wonder-ful nieces and nephews, Matt, Andy, Tyler, Tucker, Jackson, and Flavia
Love, Aunt Amy

Big thank you's and kisses to Paris Rosenthal for permission to include her poem "One of These Things Is Not Like the Other" (page 72) and to Justin Rosenthal for letting me run with his idea of a *CheF.B.I.* (page 42).
—A.K.R.

For Anna and Linda
—P.S.

10 9 8 7 6 5 4 3 2

Wonder Book

Pancake College

Saturday morning's special
There's no place I'd rather be
Than in the kitchen with Dad
Making pancake history

I don't know how he does it
But they are perfect on each side
His skillful flipping maneuvers
Make my eyes go real wide

I'll tell you where he got
All that golden-brown knowledge
My dad pulled all-nighters
While attending Pancake College

Sometimes he adds bananas
And sometimes chocolate chips
Saturday mornings I am smiling
From my heart up to my lips

My dad can make cool shapes
He can even write my name
Oh, the things he does with batter
Puts other pancakes to shame

I'll tell you how he got
His amazing short-stack knowledge
My dad graduated cum laude
From the famous Pancake College.

It Could Be Verse

Eeny Meeny and Miney Moe
Caught a tiger with their tow
The tiger hollered; they wouldn't let go
No more Eeny Meeny or Miney Moe.

Mary had a little lamp
Little lamp
Little lamp
Mary had a little lamp
Whose light was white and glowed.

Tinkle
Tinkle
In the sea
Don't look under
While I pee . . .

This little piggy played the stock market

This little piggy loved a gnome

This little piggy was a toast thief

This little piggy loved a nun.

(And the French little piggy went *Oui Oui Oui* all the way home.)

Typical Day

Can I wear pajamas to school?
> *No.*

Can I have pizza for breakfast?
> *Yes.*

Can I have dessert after I eat my pizza?
> *No.*

Can you come on the field trip next week?
> *Yes.*

Can I color on my feet?

  Yes.

Can I give the turtle a Starburst?

  No.

Can I play with Justin's toy while he's not looking?

  No.

Can I put stickers on the car?

  No.

Can I ask Madison if she can eat dinner over?

  Yes.

Can she sleep over?

  No.

Can I have this mini Baby Ruth and a candy cane?

  No.

Can I have the mini Baby Ruth and half a candy cane?

  Yes.

Can I get a monkey for my birthday?

  No.

Can I be excused?

  Yes.

Can you come upstairs with me?

  Yes.

Can I have a glass of water?

  Yes.

Can I have two more stories?

  No.

Can I have one more story?

  No.

Can you tuck me in?

  Yes.

1			
Na Napkin on lap			
2	3		
Wt Wait till all are served	**Pp** Instead of reaching say "Please pass"		
4	5	6	7
Bu Refrain from burping at table	**Pu** Refrain from passing gas at table	**Ch** Chew with mouth closed	**K** See if you can be of help in kitchen
9	10	11	12
Se When offered seconds say "Yes please" or "No thanks"	**Si** Most foods are not to be eaten with your hands—hence, silverware	**Lp** Don't just take last piece—ask if anyone else would like it	**Be** When done ask "May I be excused?

For Those Who *Periodically* Need Reminding About *Table* Manners

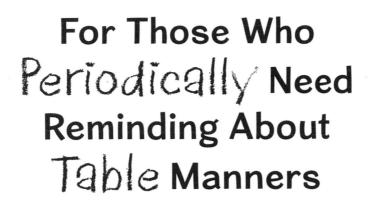

Ru

It's nice to ask How are you? How was your day?"

3

Pl

Clear your plate

Clarification

**What you
can't run with:**

Sharp pointy things

A lollipop in your mouth

Grandma's crystal swan

A truck full of scissors

A soufflé

Your shoes tied together

Twin porcupines

What you
can run with:

A bag of marshmallows

A purple sock

A napkin

A really small baby giraffe

A spoon

A kite

A friend

The Less Famous Friends of MARY MACK

Miss Mary Mellow Mellow Mellow
All dressed in yellow yellow yellow
Slept til noon noon noon
And then ate Jell-O Jell-O Jell-O

She watched her TV TV TV
All 50 channels channels channels
She was so comfy 'omfy 'omfy
In her flannels flannels flannels

Miss Mary Sue Sue Sue
All dressed in blue blue blue
Was always asked asked asked
What's with your 'do 'do 'do?

"It was the style style style
In 1950 '50 '50
You can laugh laugh laugh
But I think it's nifty nifty nifty"

Miss Mary Fred Fred Fred
All dressed in red red red
Sailed the world world world
On her sled sled sled

She flew down Everest Everest Everest
50 miles an hour hour hour
She whooshed right under under under
The Eiffel Tower Tower Tower

Miss Mary Fright Fright Fright
All dressed in white white white
Was scared of everything thing thing
On her right right right

She paid the doctor doctor doctor
50 dollars dollars dollars
But he didn't stand on her left left left
So she just hollered hollered hollered

Miss Mary Stink Stink Stink
All dressed in pink pink pink
Scrubbed her feet feet feet
In the sink sink sink

She hadn't bathed bathed bathed
In 50 weeks weeks weeks
You should see see see
Her grubby cheeks cheeks cheeks

Now you make your own . . .
Miss Mary _____
All dressed in _____
     Green
     Maroon
     Gray
     Orange (trick question)

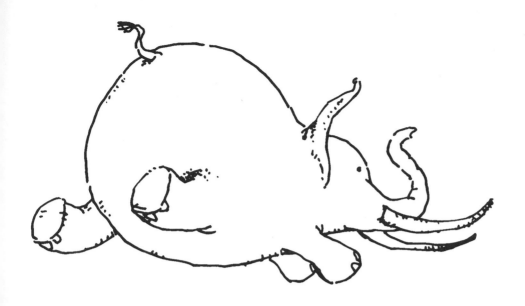

And whatever became of Miss Mary Mack, you ask?

Miss Mary Mack Mack Mack
Is still dressed in black black black
With silver buttons buttons buttons
All down her back back back

But now SHE'S the mother mother mother
And her daughter needs 50 cents cents cents
To see the elephants elephants elephants
Jump over that fence fence fence!

23

How to Avoid Stirring Up Bad Luck

Don't wok under ladders.

Prince Backwards

And to that we say, bye-good, The End.
Backwards-ly ever after they lived as true friends.
Each thought ecstatically, "I belong, I belong!"
With their backs to the wind as they strolled along,
Exactly the meal a couple backwards folks deserve.
Dessert first, then dinner, then hors d'oeuvres.
And there she appeared more beautiful than before.
"Tomorrow at five I shall be at your door."
Extend an invitation to my palace to play?"
"Forgive my forwardness, but please, if I may,
Just the kind of guy she always wanted to meet.
She was smitten not by royal face but by feet.

'Til fate bumped in, and them, into one another.
He knew not of the maiden who was unlike any other,
He was greeted by snickers, whispers, and frowns.
Backwards he galloped through forest and town.
But alas, Prince B was looking the other way.
"One day, the kingdom's yours," his dad proudly did say.
"I know, I know, I do it by choice."
"Your shoes are on backwards," many did voice.
He wore his crown backwards upon his head.
He slept completely backwards in his bed.
There lived a one-of-a-kind backwards prince
Once upon a time and never again since,

START HERE

A Rose by
Any Other Name

In Spain it's called a *pedo*
In Hungary you'd pass a *fing*
In Dutch you'd say *en wind laten*
When your bottom sings

In Japan it's called *he onara*
In Germany you'd pass *der pup*
In Italian you'd say *peto*
When that small sound erupts

In Russia it's called a *perdun*
In Hindi you'd pass a *pud*
In Polish you'd say *pierdzenic*
For both loud or quiet duds

No matter where you come from
Or what language that you speak
It's just really really funny
To hear a tushy squeak.

Take a Deep Breath . . .

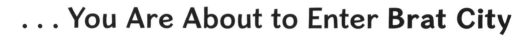

. . . You Are About to Enter Brat City

Brat City

I'll be your tour guide today
But these sites won't be pretty
So get comfy, have a seat
We're about to enter Brat City

You won't hear cars honking
Nor the clatter of fancy dining
In Brat City all you'll ever hear
Is the constant drone of whining

You'll see there are no city limits
(The parents never set them)
You'll find the kids running wild
(The parents always let 'em)

They speak their own languages here
"I WANT" is what it's called
That's how they start every sentence
Most visitors are appalled

"I want this toy now, Mother"
"But you just had your birthday, dear"
"I said I want this toy now—
You expect me to wait a year?!"

Just ahead and to your left
You can see "double stop signs"
Why are there two back to back?
'Cause no one listens the first time

We won't go inside City Hall
It's no longer a prestigious address
Toys, candy wrappers, dirty socks—
The brats refuse to clean their mess

On your right is the former site
Of the best movie theater in town
But the brats wouldn't wait in line
So they had to shut it down

True, it's a terrible city to visit
But it's an even worse place to live
Everyone takes takes takes
But no one thinks to give

So that concludes today's tour
If you someday return again
You'll find how they've all grown into
Big brat women and big brat men.

A Man, a Plan, a Canal . . . Palindromes

(A palindrome is a word or phrase that reads
the same forward and backward.)

Mom
Dad
Kayak

Was it Eliot's toilet I saw?

Too bad I hid a boot.

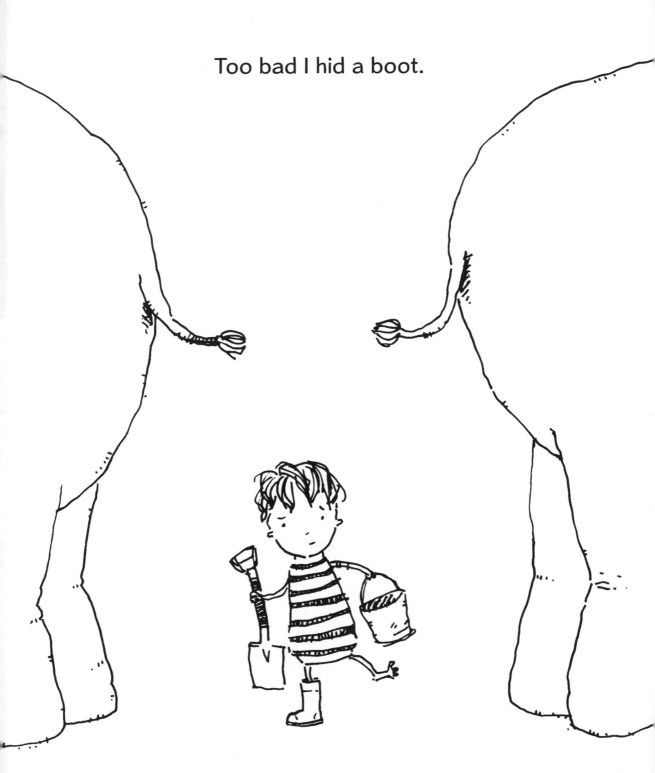

A mall llama!

Not now.

Won ton?

Today's my half birthday!
I ran right into my parent's bed.
Dad grumbled, "It's half past six."
Mom half-heartedly kissed me on the head.

I told my sister the big news.
Maybe today she won't be a pain.
But all she said was "How perfect—
Because you only have half a brain."

At school I wanted a crown.
This made my teacher laugh.
She gave me a crown all right—
Alas, she gave me half.

Mom says I should keep in mind
That the other half's coming up soon.
Then she pointed out my window. . .
There in the sky, a half moon!

HALF BIRTHDAY

Maternal Bureau
of Investigation

If you're gonna sneak a cookie
Don't act like some young rookie
Wipe up your trail of crumbs
Lick the chocolate from your thumbs
Practice "nope, not me" faces
Just to cover all your bases
See, you never know which mother
Is working undercover
'Til the moment she yells

Freeze!
CHEF.B.I.

Drop the cookie please!

Tyrannothesaurus REX:

The Dinosaur with the Killer Vocabulary

EPILOGUE:
Now you know how the dinosaurs became extinct: Tyrannothesaurus Rex (a herbivore and socialbore) simply talked everyone to death!

Week at a Glance

Sun Day

Money Day

Twos Day

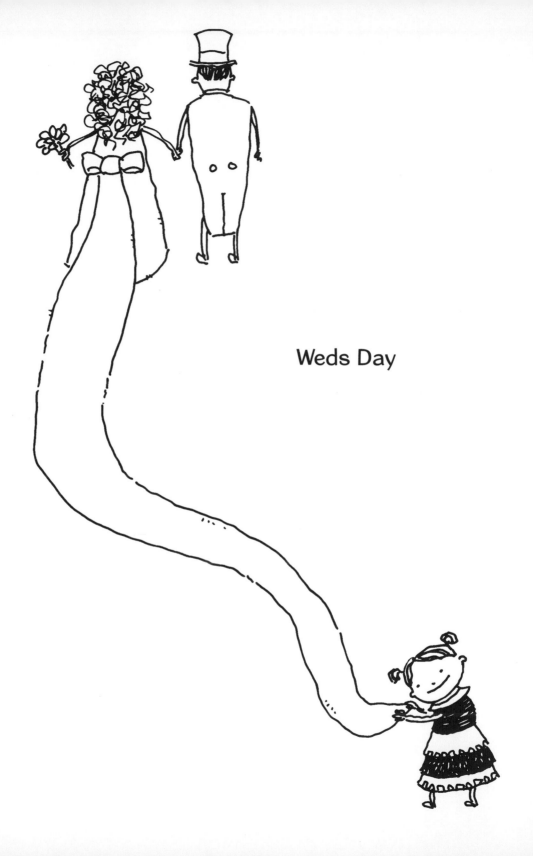

Weds Day

Thirst Day

Fry Day

Sat-on-her Day

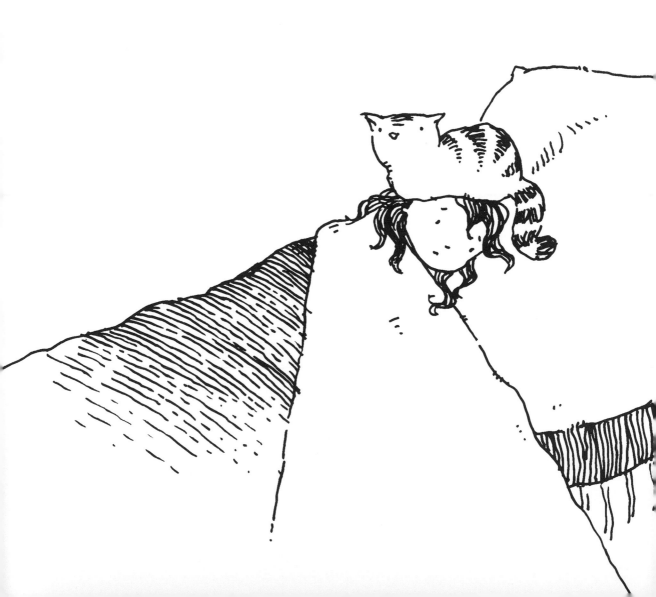

Word Play
(in Four Acts)

The bicycle couldn't stand alone
(It was two tired)

The TV couldn't sleep
(It was too wired)

The stockings couldn't stay
(They had to run)

The poem had to end
(Limit on puns)

Fifi Hockenthal
Thinks She Knows It All

Here she comes, Little Miss Know-It-All.
>*Correction, friends: The name's Miss Hockenthal.*

You think you know everything? We'll see about that.
>*I'll answer any question in three seconds flat.*

At what temperature does water freeze?
>*Everyone knows it's 32 degrees.*

How many feet are in a yard?
>*Three. Now please! Something hard.*

How much water covers the earth?
>*2/3—I've known that since birth.*

In which directions does the sun rise and set?
>*Comes up in the East, then drops in the West.*

Point to the biggest continent on the map.

Right here—Asia—that's a snap.

The Eiffel Tower stands in which city?

In Paris, France, ma petite chérie.

Who was the first president of the U.S.?

George Washington—you call this a test?

Which president put slavery to an end?

Abraham Lincoln was the one who did mend.

How many stars are on our flag?

50 allows each state to brag.

What address does the White House have?

In D.C. it's 1600 Pennsylvania Ave.

What happened in the year 1492?

Chris Columbus sailed the ocean blue.

What about later, in 1776?

The Declaration of Independence.

What did Thomas Alva Edison invent?

We have electricity thanks to that gent.

Then what about Alexander Graham Bell?

The telephone. Gosh, I'm doing well!

Who was the first American on the moon?

Neil Armstrong—I'm no buffoon.

Finish the phrase . . . "I before E . . ."

You want to talk spelling? "Except after C."

What's a fancy name for the star of a story?

"Protagonist" is the one who gets all the glory.

Name four great artists in a row.

Picasso. Pollock. Matisse. Van Gogh.

How many keys are on a piano?

With 88 you can play a concerto.

How do you say "hi" in Japanese?

Konichiwa! Sounds like a sneeze!

What's the biggest animal on land, on sea?

Elephant. Blue Whale. Can't stump me!

OK. Tomato: Vegetable or fruit?

To know it's the latter means you're astute.

I give up——there really is nothing you don't know.

Please don't make me say, "I told you so!"

Wait! Define "epidermis," as in yours is showing!

Uh, uh, uh . . .

It just means "skin" and— ahem!— now mine's glowing!

Further Clarification

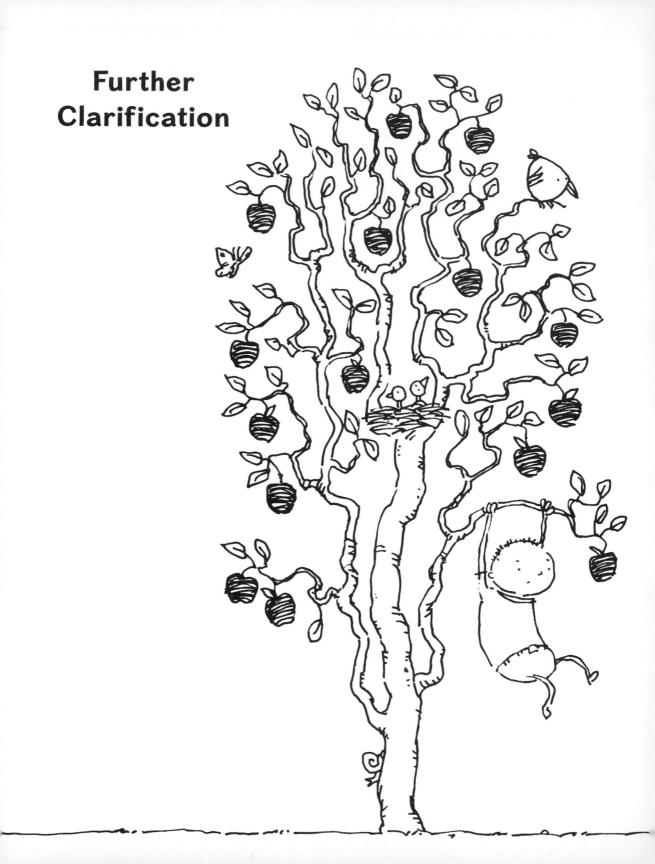

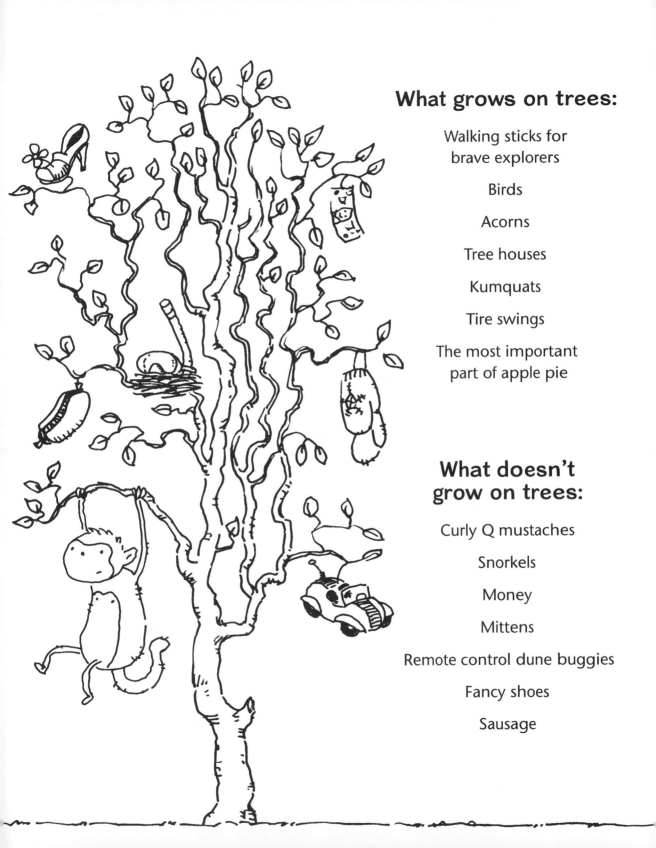

What grows on trees:

Walking sticks for
brave explorers

Birds

Acorns

Tree houses

Kumquats

Tire swings

The most important
part of apple pie

What doesn't
grow on trees:

Curly Q mustaches

Snorkels

Money

Mittens

Remote control dune buggies

Fancy shoes

Sausage

Sounds like R-U-S-T

What the boy said to the new
girl (Ester Klein) in his class:

Are you Estie?

What the British man said when he
tasted his first cup of American tea:

Arrrr!!! U.S. tea!

What the confused kindergartner said when his
teacher asked him which letters come after Q:

R-U-S-T

(Close! the U comes AFTER the T)

Stop That! Be Quiet!
Please Sit Still!

It's first thing in the morning
Class has gathered on the rug
Ms. Asher is taking roll call
J.J.'s found some braids to tug

Stop that!
Be quiet!
Please sit still!
Now is not the time for that
Can't you chill?

Friday afternoon
Off to Tae Kwon Do class
It begins with silent meditation
J.J. wants a ball to pass

Stop that!
Be quiet!
Please sit still!
Now is not the time for that
Can't you chill?

Dinner hour now
The family's at the table
Dad wants to know "How's your day?"
J.J.'s being a horse at a stable

Stop that!
Be quiet!
Please sit still!
Now is not the time for that
Can't you chill?

A special family outing
Downtown to the symphony
Time to listen, pay attention
J.J.'s busy tapping his brother's knee

Stop that!
Be quiet!
Please sit still!
Now is not the time for that
Can't you chill?

Home for stories and bed
A peaceful time for all
Mom's trying to sing sweet Mom songs
J.J.'s bouncing off the wall

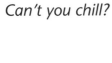

Stop that!
Be quiet!
Please sit still!
Now is not the time for that
Can't you chill?

Saturday morning stroll with Dad
They pass an old man rocking on his swing
Dad says, "Shhh, the man is resting"
But the man wants J.J. to do his thing

Oh, don't stop!
Be louder!

I am so glad that you're here!

What a lovely spirit you have!

And it brings me such cheer . . .

A Tale About Rhyming . . .
And Some Very Fortunate Timing

Once (not twice) upon a time
There lived a boy who couldn't rhyme.
"I really don't know how to do it."
His friends said, "Come on, ain't nothing to it."
He asked his mom, "Does *tree* rhyme with *boot*?"
She shook her head no. The boy cried "Shoot!"
He asked his dad, "Does *leg* rhyme with *ear*?"
His dad said, "Nope." The boy shed a tear.
He tried and tried but couldn't get it down.
Then one day a new store came to town.
When he heard about this funny new place,
A gigantic smile appeared on his face.
RHYMING STORE: RHYMES FOR GIRLS AND BOYS
"A rhyming store—that's better than toys!"
What did he see when he walked in the door?
Rhymes everywhere, from ceiling to floor!

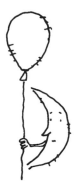

A red bed, a big wig, a blue shoe, a tall ball.
A rock sock, a white kite, a pink sink, a y'all drawl.
"I'd like the round hound, sir, but all I have is a dime."
"That will do, son; now go enjoy your new rhyme."
The boy took it home and put it on his shelf.
And now he can rhyme . . . all by _____.

One of These Things Is
Not Like the Other

Abby, Gabby,

Eddy, Teddy,

Freddy, Neddy,

Kelly, Nelly,

Haley, Kaley

Louie, Stewey

Bob.

Fruitful Love

Cantaloupe

Honeydew

Orange

Apple

Rhyming Summary
of the Universe

It's a bit of a challenge to cut a steak with a spoon.
Don't show up at 12:10 if you agreed to 12 noon.

You might be your least charming when it matters the most.
It's not a big deal when you burn your morning toast.

Ask not "What will you give me if I help you with the dishes?"
Give away two—okay, one—if you're granted three wishes.

Do the worst part of the homework first; don't save it for later.
Stand up for your sibling or some picked-on first grader.

Keep your nails, ears, and nose clean and always wear good shoes.
Use a nice firm handshake with your "Hi, how are you?"s.

Go jump in the puddle; just bring extra socks.
Think twice about flocking to where everyone else flocks.

Hang on to your old pals while making friends that are newer.
Some days your zipper will jam and your hat'll fall down a sewer.

Despite your best efforts, your goldfish may stop swimming.
It is unbecoming to always be gimme, gimme, gimme-ing.

If your neighbor is sick, bring over lollipops and soup.
Cursive takes practice, with those fancy twirls and loops.

No matter how big the cake there's only four corner pieces.
Uncles like to steal noses from nephews and nieces.

Learn how to listen (Did you hear what I said?)
When you roll a five, don't sneak six spaces ahead.

Your parents will often annoy you for no certain reason.
Enjoy blueberries while you can (they have a very short season).

64 crayons you do not really need.
To be happy with three is to be happy indeed.

Index

Key Words

Key Images

Keys

The Not-Beginning

Library of Congress catalog card number: 2008939052
ISBN 978-0-06-142974-3 (trade bdg.)
ISBN 978-0-06-142975-0 (lib. bdg.)

Typography by Dana Fritts 19 20   SCP   10 9 8 7 6 ❖ First Edition